rustam zindagi

Flairs and Glairs
Publication House

"Rustam Zindagi"

ISBN No: " 978-93-91302-54-2"
1st Edition
Language – English and Hindi

Flairs and Glairs
Publication House
Regd. Under MSME Act.

Disclaimer

This is a work of fiction and solely represent the thoughts of the corresponding authors of the articles. Our editors have tried their best to edit the content of all the authors and check the plagiarism.
All the write-ups in this book are unique and are only published in this book.
In case any plagiarism or error is found, only the author is responsible alone, and not the publisher or the Compilers.

Cover Designing and Book Formatting
Shubham Shah and Ishani Agarwal

Acknowledgment

This book "Rustam Zindagi" is a dream come true for me and my co-authours. I have always wanted to create a collection of unique and independent voices. And here I am with more than 40 co-authours from different parts of the world.

Thank you to each and every co-authours of this anthologies for their dedication, hard work, cooperation and support without which this book would have never been possible. I would also like to thank "Flairs & Glairs Publication" for giving me such a wonderful opportunity and platform through this anthology.

Co Authors

Shubham Shah (Founder Flairs and Glairs)
Ishani Agarwal (Co-Founder Flairs and Glairs)
Eram Fatma (Compiler)
Chhaya Dadhwal (Compiler)

1. Sradha Agrawal
2. Prakash Das Manikpuri
3. Dr. Rakesh R. Mund
4. Rishi Raj
5. Raj Pokhriyal
6. Bheemparam Kishor Kumar
7. Kran Das Manikpuri
8. Nikita Anand Agrawal
9. Inder Gautam
10. Sahil Ansari
11. Heera Lal Gupta
12. Umesh Panakaj[Kabir]
13. Shubham Rajwanshi
14. Megha Agarwal
15. Aman Raj
16. Sushmita Mishra
17. Bhavik Pathak
18. Shubham Tyagi
19. Salyali Das
20. Rhythm Gandhi
21. Nishigandha Das
22. Gaurangi Singh
23. Snehasish Kanungo
24. Rutuja Pardeshi
25. Upasana Borbora
26. Ekta Singh
27. Kumari Tripti

28. Arshi Gupta
29. Ayush Saxena
30. Dhivya Bharathi Arumugasamy
31. Qaima Hussain
32. Adiba
33. Rita Kakkar
34. Anamika Tiwari
35. King Idr
36. Dilip M. Bhise
37. Grishma Ninave
38. Ashish Kumar
39. Divyataa Banerjee

Shubham Shah

(Founder- Flairs and Glairs)

Shubham Shah, an entrepreneur at "Flairs & Glairs" a brand with dynamics in events organizing and cultural educational pan INDIA, is a 26yrs old guy who recently has entered the digital platform of imprinting emotions. He has initiated with his own open mic platform to help budding poets and aspiring writers under his brand named as "Teekhe Zasbaaat"

He is a commerce graduate from the Bhagalpur City of Bihar. He states Writing has impersonated him since childhood and he has now been writing for over a decade!
Cooking, on the other hand, is his passion! He also mentions, trying out new things just tickles him!
When asked sir, Why SPICY EMOTIONS?
He smiled and added, "agar jasbaat teekhe na ho toh wo jasbaat kahan" Spices are all that blends! So do his words!
As a chef, he presents to you his dish! Hot and freshly served! Taste it! Feel it! Enjoy it! You can also find his writing in the Book "Teekhe Zasbaaat" and 50+ Co-authored anthologies. With his passion to explore opportunities across Platforms, he is working with keen devotion and We wish him all the very best for his future ventures.
He is Featured in the International Magazine DeMode for his upcoming solo novel.
He is Approved by Ne8x for its Lit Fest, and is a Golden Star Awards 2020 Winner.
He is a India Book of Records Holder for his Anthology Satrang, and has the Grandmaster title by Asia Book of Records, for the same.
He has also been featured in Prabhat Khabar, Dainik Jagran, and a lot of other Newspapers in Bihar for his achievements.
He has been a proud co-author to
India Book Of Records (Title- Black)
World Book Of Records (Title -15 Wonders of Poetries)
India Book Of Records (Title - Aaina)
Vajra World Records Holder (Title - Gustakhi Maaf Hai)
High Range of Records Holder (Title - Gustakhi Maaf Hai)
Indian Book of Records
(Title - Road from Worst to Best)

Share your reviews on his

INSTAGRAM

@spicy_emotions
@shubham4shah

Or via email on

shubham2shah@gmail.com

To stay tuned to his work and opportunities follow his business Handles

INSTAGRAM FACEBOOK YOUTUBE

@flairsandglairs
@teekhezasbaaat

WEBSITE:

https://flairsandglairs.in/
https://flairsandglairs.com/

Ishani Agarwal

(Co-Founder- Flairs and Glairs)

Ishani Agarwal hails from the City of Joy, Kolkata.
She is the co-founder of her Community "Teekhe Zasbaaat" and Flairs and Glairs Publication.
Been a Compiler for 45+ Anthologies, she is in the process for more. Co-authored in 150+ Anthologies. She is a India Book of Records Holder, a Vajra World Records Holder, a High Range of Records Holder, an OMG Book of Records Holder, a Bravo Record holder, a Forever Star Book of World Records and an Indian Book of Records Holder.
Approved by Ne8x for its Lit Fest 2020, and Literary Icon 2020. Also a Golden Star Awards Winner 2020.
She has also been awarded with India Star Republic Award 2021, a part of She Awards by Awards Arc and Winner of Nari Samman 2021 by Literoma.

She is also selected as Best Achiever of the Year by AwardsArc and Most Challenging Compiler Award by Spectrum Awards.
She got her first solo Published,a solo Compilation consisting of first 750 contents of hers, titled "Hand That Burnt While Healing".

She has been featured by the National Magazine "Taree Zameen Par" with the title 'unstoppable'.
Also featured in the International Magazine DeMode for her upcoming solo novel, she is proud to write on social issues, and is happy with the love she is receiving.
Connect with her on Instagram: @Ishani_agarwal_quotes / @compilations_so_far

Eram Fatma
(Compiler)

Author Eram Fatma was born in Bihar (Patna), is fond of writing and has started her own writing page on Instagram called "thewingsof_blossom", she has co-authored in many anthologies and is in the process for more, she has been writing for two years But recently decided to step into the world of publishing.

Instagram id: thewingsof_blossomsblossom

Lost Me

I and my loneliness were looking up at the sky,
And was counting the stars.

I was trying to wrap my broken heart.
That night was very dark and grossly quiet.

My soul is screaming in the thundering night.
Hiding behind all my worries with a smile
of expression.

And these things were killing me inside.
The desire to take a long tight hug,
so that all my sorrows go away.

Somehow I hope for a new beginning,
where I now feel that nothing is left.

And I have to rebuild myself.
Now I want to greet my reflection
instead of looking at the past.

And want to promise to love myself
a little more everyday.

कुछ अनकही बातें

कुछ बातें अभी बाक़ी है,
कुछ मुलाकातें अभी बाक़ी है

कुछ ज़िंदगी के उलझे हुए धागे हैं
जिन्हें सुलझाना अभी बाक़ी है|

कुछ फिक्र, हक़, मोहब्बत, ज़िद...
तुझ पर जताना आभी बाकी है|

चल आ दो पल बैठ मुझ संग,
कुछ बेवजह के वहम मिटाने आभी बाकी है|

चल कुछ पुरानी यादें समेट कर
एक नया किस्सा बनाते हैं ,

क्योंकि कुछ राहों की तलाश ,
तुझ संग अभी करनी बाकी है|

Chhaya Dadhwal (Compiler)

She is Chhaya Dadhwal ,belongs to Hamirpur , Himachal Pradesh. Presently ,she is pursuing her PhD (Economics) at NIT Hamirpur . Her hobbies are yog , listening music , reading books and Writing.She is a passionate researcher as well as writer , Published her poetry in E-Magazine and 5 anthologies. She like spend her free time by singing , sports and talking to friends .She is a happy soul , living a simple life and modern thought.

यह ज़िन्दगी क्या है ?
रहस्य ....
हमारा जीवन 'प्रेम' से जीवित है,
या हमारे प्रेम में 'जीवन'है ।

हम जीवन भर प्रेम का इंतज़ार करते हैं।
हमे वास्तव में प्रेम नही मिलता है या हम
क़बूल नही करते है ।
जब हमें प्रेम मिला, उस वक़्त हमे प्रेम की
तवज्जो न थी।

और फिर जब हमें समझ आयी ,कि प्रेम
मिल रहा है तो हम ज़िन्दगी का और
इंतज़ार करते है।

असल में हम अपनी ज़िंदगी को मतलब के
ज़रिए से जीते हैं, किंतु अगर जीना ज़रिया
हो, तो यही जिंदगी का असल मतलब है ।

इस 'रुस्तम' ज़िन्दगी में क्या है ?
इस ज़िन्दगी में सब कुछ 'प्रेम' है और यह
प्रेम ही रुस्तम ज़िन्दगी है ।

Sradha Agrawal

This is Sradha Agarwal, she is a student by profession. She lives in a beautiful state called Sikkim the climate there is mild and moderate. She is new to writing and have started it from last 5 months.

She loves travelling to new places, clicking pictures of those places, she likes music a lot since she thinks that music helps her restore her soul. And now even writing is one of her hobbies. She said that she was motivated by her friend and her family members who supported her to write more. She also wants support from others as well so that she can improve her write up.

Email : shradhaagarwal32@gmail.com
Follow on Instagram ID- @_sophia._11

Enhance Your Inner Beauty

People with pretty faces look so pleasant and attractive but mostly they are arrogant and carry a lot of attitude with them. Nowadays people have started appreciating the outer beauty of people so much which has made the inner beauty lost somewhere. Rather than the talent of people their beauty is judged. The thing which should be the most appreciated one is the inner beauty because no one knows what may happen to the outer beauty since it eventually will get faded away but the inner one always remains.

"COLOUR" What does this word define?

This is something which should never be used to describe a person because we don't hold any right to describe anyone by their colour.

Why don't people understand? The thing we should consider first is the inner beauty, we should see whether that person is caring or not, we should see how helpful they are for the needy, we should see what has the person done for the society. This makes a person beautiful both from inside and outside.

Let's learn to be beautiful from inside rather than showing it on our faces which will eventually lose its value.

Beautiful Friendship

She came to her life suddenly, even though they were stranger but yet there was a connection. They saw each other daily and then, finally after 4 months they conversed with each other. Then they exchanged their mobile numbers and became friends. They studied together and gave their 10th board exams. Soon the results was out. They were not together that time but yet were thinking about each other. As soon reached home they contacted each other for the results and were really happy for each other. But after that they got apart into different streams and studied in different schools. For few months it was quite difficult but they managed to do it and even kept their relation safe. They reached class 12 and missed each other so finally they made a plan to meet. They met in the evening time near their house and talked the whole evening about school and how was life going on, they were really happy after meeting each other. As it was turning dark they got back to their houses and then texted that they should meet frequently. Then they promised to support each other and remain side by side in any difficulty.

This maybe just a story for others but it is a true-life story of two friends. Although it's short but yet it can define their beautiful friendship.

प्रकाश दास मानिकपुरी

मेरे कॉलेज के समय एक बार मेरे मित्रों के साथ कवि सम्मेलन देखने गया था तब से मुझे कविताओं की ओर रुझान आया। मैंने लेखन का कार्य वर्ष 2016 से प्रारंभ किया। अपने लेखन के शुरुआती समय में मैंने श्रृंगार की कविताएं लिखना शुरू किया लेकिन बाद स्तिथि को देखते हुए हास्य लेखन भी शुरू किया और श्रृंगार में हास्य लिखने का प्रयास किया जो कि एक सफल प्रयास रहा।

Email : pracky.mnpuri56@gmail.com

Instagram ID:- @poet_prakash

तुम मुझसे प्यार तो करते हो पर जताते नहीं हो

अपने दिल की बातों को होठों तक लाते नहीं हो,
तुम मुझसे प्यार तो करते हो पर जताते नहीं हो।

पहली बार जो तुमको देखा तुम थोड़ी सकुचाई थी,
प्यार था दिल में तेरे तब तो अगले दिन मिलने आई थी,
समझ जाते हो दिल की बातें पर क्यों बताते नहीं हो?
तुम मुझसे प्यार तो करते हो पर जताते नहीं हो।

कुछ दिन तुमसे दूर रहा था मेरी परीक्षा की बारी थी,
दिल के जंग में लेकिन तुमने पक्की बाज़ी मारी थी,
बड़ी भोली हो दिल की, मुझसे कुछ भी छुपाते नहीं हो,
तुम मुझसे प्यार तो करते हो पर जताते नहीं हो।

साथ नहीं रहता ज्यादा दिन, जो जान से प्यारा होता है,
पाता है किसी का साथ तो वो फिर,साथ किसी का खोता है,
कहीं मेरा दिल दुःख न जाए, करके सताते नहीं हो,
तुम मुझसे प्यार तो करते हो पर जताते नहीं हो।

रसोई तुमको प्रिय बहुत है, पकवान बनाना भाता है,
कौन सा ऐसा काम है बोलो, तुम्हें नहीं जो आता है,
मैं जब तेरे साथ रहूँ तो, बिना मेरे कुछ खाते नहीं हो,
तुम मुझसे प्यार तो करते हो पर जताते नहीं हो।

एक मासूम की आँखों में

असुरक्षा का डर है देखो एक मासूम की आँखों में,
उम्मीदों का घर है देखो एक मासूम की आँखों में।

किस पर वो विश्वास करे अब किसको वो अपना माने,
कोई नहीं जो उसको समझे किसको वो अपना जाने।
आँख मूंद कर किया भरोसा सोचा मेरा अपना है,
पर उसने ही धूल झोंक दी एक मासूम की आँखों में।।

बाहर जाना बंद हो गया अब जाए तो जाए कैसे,
ये मुझको अपना जानेगा खुद को समझाए कैसे।
खुद में डरी सहमी सी देखो कैसे कुछ भी कह पाए,
कोई ना सम्मान बचा जब एक मासूम की आँखों में।।

असुरक्षा का डर है देखो एक मासूम की आँखों में,
उम्मीदों का घर है देखो एक मासूम की आँखों में।

दोषी उसको कहे जमाना इसमें उसका दोष कहाँ,
अपने वो सम्मान के खातिर दर दर भागे यहाँ-वहाँ।
गलती उस हैवान ने की तो सज़ा इसे क्यूँ देते हो,
कोई तो उम्मीद जगाओ एक मासूम की आँखों में।।

कोई ना सम्मान करे ना कोई अपनाये उसको,
कोई नहीं जो साथ रहे ना कोई हक दिलाये उसको।
लड़ लड़कर वो टूट चुकी है अब और करे वो क्या बोलो,
निराशा का बस भाव है दिखता एक मासूम की आँखों में।।

संग उसके परिवार है पिसता दुर्व्यवहार के चक्की में,
कहीं से फटता कहीं से घिसता बदले की एक अग्नि में।
आओ मिल संकल्प करें हम साथ हैं वीरांगनाओं के,
एक उम्मीद का दीप जलाएं एक मासूम की आँखों में।।

Dr Rakesh R Mund

Dr Rakesh R Mund has been participating in more than *50 anthologies*. His educational background has given broad base which represents medical and scientific topics. He funds to read Veda and different literatures which give a glimpse on his writing. You can contact with him.

Email : Rakeshranjanmund.rrm1@gmail.com

Instagram ID- @Rakeshmundr_

कैसे कहें ?

परास्त हो गया इश्क
करने वाला,
जीत गया वो हिज्र में
अपनाने वाला,
नियति भी ऐसी क़हर
क़यामत दिन लाए,
अकेले कष्ट क्यों झेलें हम
कारवाँ साथ लाए ।

प्राण से ज्यादा प्रेम करने की
प्रण था तुम्हारा,
शांत हृदय में आग लगाके अशांत
हुआ मन हमारा,
जल रहे हैं हम दहकती बेवफाई
तुमने जो दीया,
तुम थी इतनी मनमोहनी खुशी से
दर्द हमने लिया ।

वादा निभाने में हो तकलीफ तो
आगोश में क्यों लिया ?
तुम चले गये नये नये बाहोँ में
हमें यादोँ में तड़पाया !
सर्पों के दंशन से जिंदा रेह लिए
ये धोकाधड़ी में कैसे रहें ?
तुम हो हिज्र के दवाई हम अश्कों
में तड़पते अब कैसे कहे.

ऋषि राज

ऋषि राज (राज आर.) चंडीगढ़ से हैँ और दवा बनाने वाली मल्टीनेशनल कंपनी में काम करते हैं। हिंदी और पंजाबी में लिखते है। इन के लिखे कुछ भजन टी-सीरीज द्वारा भी रिलीज़ किये गए है। इन्होंने समाजिक समस्याओं पे कई कविताएं लिखी हैं। इनकी दो रचनाएँ इस क़िताब में प्रकाशित की जा रही हैं और हमें पूरी उम्मीद है कि आप को पसंद आएँगी।

Email : rishiraj.agnihitri@rediffmail.com

ख़बर चुनाव की

शेरों ने उपवास रखे हैं हिरण बचाने की कसमें खाई हैं
जब से खबर चुनाव की आई है,
खबर चुनाव की आई है
लंबे चौड़े दे दे भाषण हजम कर रहे खाया राशन
नेताओं की फौज को देखो अब करने चली भलाई है
हर पिछड़ा है साथी इनका हर गरीब अब भाई है
जब से खबर चुनाव की आई है,
खबर चुनाव की आई है
एक दूजे को झूठा कहते, खुद को कहते सच्चा
ना ही अनपढ़ आज का वोटर, ना ही है वो बच्चा
सबक सीखाने की अबके मन में वोटर के आई है
जब से खबर चुनाव की आई है,
खबर चुनाव की आई है
जात पात पे बांटा है कहीं लालच दिया है चोखा
वादे करते बड़े-बड़े पर देंगे बस ये धोखा
मुद्दा कर कोई गरम पुराना धर्म के नाम पर आग लगाई है
जब से खबर चुनाव की आई है
खबर चुनाव की आई
झांसे में कहीं आ ना जाना इनके
बदले लेना तुम भी गिन गिन के
पैसे लेकर वोट जो दोगे
आने वाली नस्लों को क्या मुंह दोगे
कल तक था नहीं जिन्हें राशन मिलता
उन्हें जा रही शराब पिलाई है
जब से खबर चुनाव की आई है,
खबर चुनाव की आई है.

नफ़रत फ़ैलती कैसे है

तुम समझ पा रहे क्या
नफ़रत फैलती कैसे है
बड़ा आसान है उन के लिए
जिनका काम फैलाना है
तुम तो बस मोहरे हो
हो रहे हो जो क़ुर्बान
वो देते उकसा तुम को
कर के बातें बड़ी बड़ी
कोई ज़ाती मक़सद है उनका
पूरा करवा रहे है तुम से जो
दिखा के मंज़िल और कोई
ले जाएंगे और कहीं
वहाँ होगा पछतावा
नहीं होगा वक़्त गया
बच्चे जलेंगे जब ज़िंदा
वजह तुम्ही होगे
दर्द यतीमों के की
वजह तुम्ही होगे
हो गी बेवा जब मजबूर कोई
तो वजह तुम्ही होगे
जो भी होगा इकतरफ़ा नहीं होगा
हशर तो यही होगा
कहीं ज़्यादा तो कहीं कम होगा
पर वजह तुम्ही होगे
आँखे मूंद लो चाहे तुम
ख़ुद को कर लो साबित कितना
पर सच तब भी वही होगा
तुम्हारी रूह चीख़ के कहती जो
बस सच वही होगा

राज पोखरियाल

सहलेखक का नाम राजेन्द्र प्रसाद है उनका प्रचलित नाम राज पोखरियाल है। वह पहाड़ी राज्य उत्तराखंड पौडी जनपद के मूल निवासी है। उनकी शिक्षा स्नातक स्तर तक उत्तराखंड के हेमवती नंदन बहुगुणा कॉलेज से हुई है । इनकी रूचि पढ़ाई के साथ लेखन में शुरू से ही है। इन्होंने अपना लेखन कार्य स्कूल शिक्षा के दौरान ही शुरू कर दिया था। वर्तमान काल में एक कंपनी में मैनेजर के पद पर कार्यरत हैं।

Email : patonrpp@gmail.com

Instagram ID
Raj_pokhriyal

"मै लिखता हूँ"

मै लिखता हूँ ,तेरे ख्याल में !
मै लिखता हूँ ,अपने ख्याल से !

शायद मतलब न हो, शब्द अर्थहीन हो,
शब्द वजनी न हो ,रचनात्मक न हो
काव्यात्मक न हो, भावात्मक न हो

फिर भी मै लिखता हूँ ......
मै लिखता हूँ मेरे,शौक के लिए
मनोभाव के लिये ,आन्नद के लिये
शुकून के लिये ,समाज के लिये
प्रेम के लिए ,स्नेह के लिए
सदभाव के लिए,स्वभाव के लिये

मै लिखता हूँ,....
अपनी पीड़ा के लिए,अपनी बैचैनी के लिए
अपने दर्द के लिए ,अपने भाव के लिए
अपनी पहचान के लिए,अपने स्वाभिमान के लिये

मै लिखता हूँ ......
मै तुम्हे समझता हूँ,फिर तुम्हे लिखता हूँ
सकल संचार से ,अपने विचार से
तेरी चाह भी लिखता हूँ ,तेरी आह भी लिखता हूँ
तेरे कर्म भी लिखता हूँ ,तेरा जीवन भी लिखता हूँ
हाँ, मै तुम्हे भी लिखता हूँ

मै लिखता हूँ ...
तेरे ख्याल में

अपने ख्याल से ।।
मुझे नशा कलम का,
रंग स्हाई में डूब सा।
शब्द बने मित्र मेंरे,
ये नशा शब्दों का।।
फिर आसन बन जाता सफर
किताबों से मिलने का।

चलो न साथ चलते है,
आवो हिन्दी से मिलते है।
जो भूल रहे मात्र भाषा
उनसे भी मिलते है।।
ये मन के ख्याल को
मै तो लिख चुका हूँ
मै लिखता हूँ ....

Bheemparam Kishore Kumar

Bheemparam Kishore Kumar,
Even though by profession is a Medico at Kakatiya Medical College, Warangal. he is one among the passionate writer coming up with his talent fresh words. The way he frame his lines perfectly go in sync with the content. He has worked as Co-author for 6 anthologies.
He is always thankful to his friends & family as they in each step supported in writing in improving himself.

"He believes the art of saving lives inspires in making art of everything he can. When you feel the things happening around you, every word you speak can be made an art of it."

Email : bheemparam.kishore@gmail.com
Instagram ID
@Words_of_bheemparam

Puncturing the akward Silence
This Night with fears
He walked upto Stairs
Looking at the Clouded Sky.
With sweaty palms even at Monsoon Nights,
He Screamed Out of Agony.

Wakeup
My Girl,
It 2.00 Am Midnight
Hold My Hand My darling
& lets explore the Unexplored world.
The twinkling stars & the shining Moon
Are waiting for Us,
To meet the Beauty of the Darkness
& feel the MidNight Vibes

Oh god!
I didn't know it was she,
But the moment I realized
she was the girl who drew,
My shining Moon in the midnight Sky.

If time was a toy in My hands
I would have gone back for a while
Stop at the second where You crossed My way.

Karan Das Manikpuri

करण दास मानिकपुरी, रायगढ़ (छ.ग.) के रहने वाले है। इन्होंने बी.एस.सी. की शिक्षा प्राप्त की है। का॑लेज के दिना॓ं से ही इन्हें शेरो-शायरी में रूचि है तथा साथ ही यें संगीत में काफी रूचि रखते है।

Email : manikpuri2211@gmail.com
Instagram ID
@karan_das_manikpuri

पहली मुलाक़ात

देखा तुझे पहली दफा, एक सादगी सी झलक दिखी तुझमे।
आसपास और कुछ न दिखा बस ख़ामोशी सी दिखी तुझमे।।

दफ़अतन देखने की ख्वाहिश जाने कहा से आ गई मुझको।
पीछे छिपकर दिवार के मुसलसल देखने लगा था तुझको।

वक्त गुजरा, नाम भी जाना और समय रहते तेरा काम भी जाना।
बारिश ऐसा हुआ जाते व़क्त तेरे, लगा जैसे ख़ुदा ने मेरा हाल भी जाना।।

पर थी क्या हालात तेरे जो बारिश में जाने का ख़्याल हुआ।
मुरझाया सा चेहरा, आँखों में थोड़ा आब, ऐसा मेरा हाल हुआ।।

थी ऐसी जुनूननियत के सायकल में तुम्हारे पीछे हम भागते ही रह गये।
पर तुम्हारी थी मोटरसायकल और मेरी सायकल, फिर क्या पीछे ही रह गये।।

दूसरी मुलाकात

वो दौर भी आ गया जिसका मुझे इंतजार था।
क्लासेस भी खुल गई बचा सिर्फ तेरा ही दीदार था।।

पर हुआ क्या था तुम्हें जो नहीं आई तुम।
मन में ख़्याल आया कहीं बिमार न हो तुम।।

कुछ दिन यूं ही बीत गये पर आई नहीं तुम।
लगा जैसे यहां दाखिला करवाई नहीं तुम।।

फिर मन काफी हो गया उदास मेरा।
लगा जैसे हो गया पूरा सत्यानाश मेरा।।

क्लास में बस एक नारी थी बाकी सब थे नर।
मेरी हालत हुई खराब तो हम चले गये घर।।

जब लौटे हम तो दोस्तो की बातों से लगा आज मेरी शामत आई है।
जब क्लास के अंदर जाके देखा पता चला आज वो आई है।।

आँखें मेरी चमकने लगी और ये दिल फिर से धड़कने लगा।
पीछे बैठकर क्लास में बस उसे मैं मुसलसल तकने लगा।।

पता न चला कब सुबह से शाम हो गई।
दीदार में उसके मेरी हर चीज़ खो गई।।

क्लास के बाद वो अपने बस का इंतज़ार कर रही थी।
और ये कम्बख़्त आँखें मेरी बस उसे ही तक रही थी।।
वो वक्त आया जब वो बस में बैठकर चले गई।
और जाते हुए दिल भी मेरा लेकर चले गई।।

आज चेहरे पर एक अलग खुशी छाई थी।
मेरी ख़्वाहिश आज का◌ॅलेज जो आई थी।।

Nikita Anand Agarwal

Nikita A. Agarwal a.k.a "*zaalim*" is an engineering college dropout from Odisha. After having spent most of her life in kantabanji, a very small town in Odisha, she is currently based in Siliguri.

She expresses her thoughts when Nikita is not running here and there into her household chores.

She has been a part of various anthologies in the past as co-author.

Email : nikitaaagarwal21@gmail.com

. Instagram ID @Soulwriters81

मैं एक अदना-सा शायर

मैं एक अदना-सा शायर हूँ जनाब़
बस अपने अल्फ़ाज पिरोता हूँ..;
श्याही को ही रंग मानकर
काग़ाज पर उनको भरता हूँ..;
अख़बार की सुर्ख़ियों से परे
मैं अपना अलग संसार बसाता हूँ...
इक अधुरा-सा आश़िक नहीं मैं
बस किस्मत का मैं मारा हूँ..;
मैं कुछ़ और नहीं 'ज़ालिम'
बस एक अदना-सा शायर हूँ...!! यूँ आवारा कहकर मुझे बदनाम
ना किया करो तुम,
यूँ नकारा सोचकर तसल्लि ना दिया करो..,
बस ख़यालों में डूबा हुआ एक ख़ामोश सितारा हूँ...,
'ज़ालिम' मैं कुछ और नहीं बस एक अदना-सा शायर हूँ...!! तन्हाई
को मैं लिखता हूँ माँ की ममता दिखलाता हूँ..,
आश़िकों की आश़की लिखता हूँ अपराध की दास्तान बतलाता हूँ..,
दुनिया से रू-ब-रू तुमको मैं करवाता हूँ
मैं बस एक अदना-सा शायर हूँ...।

Keep Trying

So sad I was when I was lost
Lost in the crowds of thousands...
I never knew how to face the world
I hide myself in the crowd
And I never gave up trying...
When my old memories knocked the door
The footsteps of my parents were being heard...,
When I woke up from my dreams
Sadness followed me ever
Still,
I never gave up trying....

And then the day came
I was in the park with street children
Picking up rags and thrash
And then I saw them...my parents

But again, they were lost somewhere
Somewhere in the crowd of thousands
But, even now I am
Trying
Trying to find them out...!!

Inder Gautam

He is Inder Gautam who is co-author, author, blogger, poet and lyricist...Shy by nature, neither introvert nor extrovert but ambivert and text overt as well... Love to Reading books that's why he made himself as an....

Email : indergautam1998@gmail.com
Instagram ID
https://instagram.com/indergautam?igshid=oualzrigsjyo

रूह का रंग

तुमने मुझसे जो सवाल किया था उसका आज जवाब मिला है, बताना तो मिल के चाहता था पर इतने वक़्त बाद पता नहीं तुम सुनोगी भी या नहीं और मझे पता भी नही है तुम हो कहाँ इसलिए ये खत लिख के बताना पड़ रहा है और ये तुम्हारे उसी पते पे भेज रहा हूँ, अगर ये पढ़ पाओ तुम तो....

लाल और गुलाबी रंग को मिलाने के बाद जो रंग बनता है उसमें नीले आसमान का रंग... वो नीले असमान का रंग जिसमें पंछी बिना डरे, बेखौफ़ उड़ते हैं अपने ख़्वाबों को पूरा करने की चाहत में और वो बारिश की बूंदों से गीली हुई मिट्टी की ख़ुशबू, उस ख़ुशबू के एहसास के लिए वो बारिश की बूंदों से भीगी हुई मिट्टी का रंग... और फिर उसपे रात की चांदनी का रंग, वो चांदनी जो धीरे धीरे बढ़ती है और रात को गहरा करती चली जाती है... और इन सब पे सूरज की वो पहली किरण के तेज को मिलाने के बाद का रंग... मेरे ख़्याल से तब जाकर प्यार का रंग बनता है, ये ऐसा है जो शायद ही किसी ने देखा हो।
और इन सब को मिलाओ तो जो रंग बनता है वो तुम्हारी रूह का रंग है और मुझे कोई हर्ज़ नहीं ये कहने में की मैं इस रूह के रंग से प्यार करता हूँ, पर शायद तुम किसी और से प्यार करती हो और अगर नहीं भी करती हो तब भी मैं इतना तो जानता हूँ कि मुझसे तो हरगिज़ नहीं करती।

मुझे याद है मैंने तुम्हें अपने दिल के बारे में बताया था, तुम इस दिल को कैसी लगती हो ये भी बताया था, और आज सात साल, सात महीने, पंद्रह दिन बीत चुके हैं, तुम्हें तो शायद याद भी ना हो कि कितने बीत चुके है। तुम्हें पता भी नहीं है कि मैं तुमसे बात करने के तरीके ढूंढता रहता हूँ मग़र कभी कभी, कभी कभी क्या हमेशा ही इस डर से रुक जाता हूँ कि कहीं मेरी वज़ह से तुम परेशान ना हो

जाओ। शायद मैं ग़लत सोचता हूँ, या शायद सही भी सोचता हूँ। इन सालों में इतना उलझ गया हूँ कि मुझे समझ नहीं आता दिमाग की सुनु या दिल कि। उस दिन जब तुमने सामने से मुझसे कहा था कि आज मैंने एक सपना देखा और सपने में तुम आये थे गौतम, उस दिन मैं तुम्हें बताना चाहता था कि मेरी ख़ुशी का कोई ठिकाना नहीं था, मेरी ख़ुशी का ठिकाना नहीं था इसकी दो वज़ह थी, पहली ये की तुम्हारे ख़्वाबों के किसी हिस्से में आया था मैं, इसी बहाने तुमने मेरे बारे में सोचा तो सही और दूसरी वज़ह मैं बता नहीं सकता क्योंकि अगर मैं दूसरी वज़ह बताऊंगा तो तुम्हें शायद बुरा लगेगा और मैं नहीं चाहता मेरी वज़ह से तुम्हें ज़रा भी बुरा लगे। अब मिलना तो पता नहीं कब होगा, होगा भी या नहीं कुछ नहीं पता, और तुम मुझसे प्यार भी नहीं करती, पर दिल कहता है की तुम प्यार करती हो, मैं बस इतना चाहता हूँ कि हम जब मिलें तो वो जो तस्वीर हमने ली थी वो लेकर आना, मैं तुम्हारी तरफ़ से हाँ समझूँगा, वरना तुम मत आना क्योंकि फ़िर तुम मना करने के लिए आओगी और मैं तुम्हारी तरफ़ से अब ना सुनना नहीं चाहता। तुम्हारी अगर हाँ है और हम फिर भी ना मिल पाएं तो बस किसी तरह मुझे बता देना, बाकी तुम्हें तो पता ही है मैं तुम्हें कहाँ मिलूंगा। और में बता दूं वो तस्वीर मैंने आज भी संभाल के रखी है, और मैं उम्मीद करता हूँ तुमने भी संभाल के रखी होगी।

Sahil Ansari

Love writing the ideas, thoughts, experiences and crafting into poetry.

Email : sahilansari66435@gmail.com
Instagram ID
Wordsbyheart12(Sahilansari)

1.**Feel Like Writing...**

I feel like writing ever time
Because paper have more patience than people.

2. Growing Old Together

The sun,
who burns and dies,
for the Moon to rise.

3. The Frame In My Desk

I had kept a frame into my desk,
Waiting for you to come and love me back,
But in this journey of patience.
I forgot that expectations hurt.
But waiting is not bad since i found the result, the frame turns even more Darker

4. For Me It's Important To.

Pause and look the way back where,
I have reached now,
without you …
When I used to say that my life without you... is Meaningless.
Then …
Just waiting for you
to come back so ,…
We could walk together.

जागो, देखो

तुम ठहरे हो ,
और तुम्हारी मंज़िल आगे बढ़ रही है ।
तुम कहाँ थे ,
और कहाँ पहुंच गए,
लोग क्या कहते हैं?
अब ये फ़र्क नही पड़ता ।
मगर उनकी बात अब सच हो रही है कि,
तुम से ना हो पाएगा ।

****

मगर ये सच नही ..
मैं मरने की ख़्वाहिश से जीता हूँ हर रोज़,
मगर ये सच है
मैं मरता हूँ जीने की ख़्वाहिश से हर रोज़।

****

तुम्हें क्या हुआ है ?
अब इतना हँसने पर भी मुस्कुराते नही,
कहीं तुम्हारा मन भर तो नही गया..
इस मोहब्बत के शिकंजे से,
जो हुआ अछा हुआ।
हमे भी अब रुलाने पर आँसू नही आते।

****

मगर ये सच नही ..
मैं मरने की ख़्वाहिश से जीता हूँ हर रोज़,
मगर ये सच है
मैं मरता हूँ जीने की ख़्वाहिश से हर रोज़।
बेवफ़ा कौन है ?

अनजान है वो ,अपने फैसले से
बेख़बर है वो ,अपने किरदार से
कोई समझता है ,क्यूँ नही उसे
सिर्फ तराशते ही हैं ,क्यूँ उसे सभी

हीरालाल गुप्ता

हीरालाल गुप्ता जी, पिता श्री बलराम रायगढ़ (छ.ग.) के रहने वाले हैं। इन्होनें डीएड, हिन्दी तथा संस्कृत में स्नातकोत्तर की उपाधि प्राप्त की है, यें एक योग प्रशिक्षक भी हैं, इनका उद्देश्य योग का प्रचार तथा हिन्दी साहित्य की सेवा करना है, यें कविता, कहानी, नाटक, उपन्यास आदि के लेखन में रुचि रखते हैं, इन्होनें कई कवि सम्मेलनों में हिस्सा लिया है। प्रस्तुत पुस्तक में इन्होनें अपनी कविता में खुद की कल्पना का एक शानदार दृश्य पेश किया है।

Email : heeragupta592@gmail.com
Instagram ID @heeralal.gupta.54

हमारा पर्यावरण

चिड़ियों की चहक नहीं रही,
फूलों में महक नहीं रही......

बिना पेड़, बिना पौधों के,
जीवन संभव कैसे होगा,
बिना जननी के शिशु का,
जन्म संभव कैसे होगा,
बिना फल,बिना फूल के,
यह जीवन कांटे जैसे होगा......

होंगे पेड़ तो हरियाली होगी,
चहूं ओर खुशहाली होगी....

शुद्ध वायु,शुद्ध जल मिलेगा,
जीवन में खुशियों का पल मिलेगा,
संतुष्टि मिलेगा वर्तमान में,
नई पीढ़ी को सुन्दर कल मिलेगा....

अपने लिए नहीं तो,
अपने संतान के लिए सही,
मन में सच्चा भाव जगाएं,
चलो हम पर्यावरण बचाएं,
मिलकर कुछ पौधे लगाएं,
चलो हम संसार को,
एक सुंदर संसार बनाएं....

आओ हम पौधे लगाएं.....
आओ हम पौधे लगाएं.....

दीवाने आजादी के

हिंदुस्तां की आजादी का ,
स्वर्ण अक्षरों से लिख दी कहानी..

झूलने को थे तैयार फांसी पर,
लेकिन हार कभी ना मानी......

मौत करती रही इंतजार बाहें फैलाकर,
जैसे हो वह इनकी दीवानी.......

तोड़कर बेड़ी भारत माता के पैरों की,
कर गए देवी को स्वतंत्र रानी......

नहीं भूले हैं राजगुरु,सुखदेव,भगत जी !
हमें याद है आपकी बलिदानी....
हमें याद है आपकी बलिदानी.....

Umesh Pankaj [Kabir]

One who always believe in being empowered and being fearless, he thinks that keep trying hard even if the life gives you thousands of setbacks. Don't divided the society on the bases of caste, religion, gender, ideology etc.try to treat everyone equally. He is also express love feelings with beautifully.

Instagram: Poem_my_life_by_kabir
Email: kabirpankaj92@gmail.com

ग़ालिब

कोई महल नहीं..
टूटा-फूटा घर हो चाहे... ग़ालिब !
तस्वीर मेरी चाहे गन्दी हो,
पर पल्लू से पोंछे जो,वो बस वो हो... ग़ालिब !!
..
इत्मीनान से रख लूंगा मैं भी,
जो व्रत उसका हो,चाहे जो हो... ग़ालिब !
मैं कई दिनों तक भूखा रह लूंगा,
बस खिलाने वाला हाथ,उसका ही हो.. ग़ालिब !!
..
उसकी उड़ती जुल्फें बहुत है,
तू तूफान की बातें ना कर... ग़ालिब !
मरना है तो,उसका जाना बहुत है,
तू खंजर,हतियार की बात ना कर... ग़ालिब !!
..
गुस्ताखी उसकी कितनी भी हो,
हर-पल बस प्यार बढ़ता रहें... ग़ालिब !
शक ना हो,मोहताज ना रहें वो,
रफा-दफ़ा हर बात रहें... ग़ालिब.. !!
..
हुस्न चाहे वो कितना भी बदले,
दिल बस ये ही रखे,जिसमें मैं हूँ.. ग़ालिब..!
समय चाहे फिर कितना भी बदले,
हम दोनों ऐसे ही रहें..जैसे है.. ग़ालिब...!!

उसका होना बहुत है

मेरे ज्यादा अरमान नहीं,बस एक ख़्वाब है,
डूबते को तिनका,मुझे उसका झुमका बहुत है...
..
कोई शाम नहीं,उसकी एक मुलाक़ात ठीक है,
जैसे चकोर को चाँद,मुझे उसका दीदार बहुत है...
..
खुशनुमा मौसम नहीं,जुल्फें बस वो खोल दे,
जैसे जलते होये पतंगें को,एक दीया बहुत है...
..
लाली आसमां की नहीं,उसके होंठ ही बहुत है,
मेघों का क्या करना,उसके कजराले नैन बहुत है..
..
मुझे अप्सराओ,मलिकाओ से क्या मतलब है,
एक उसका हुस्न,एक उसका,मेरा होना बहुत है...
..
ज़िस्म की चाहत नहीं,रूह की गुजारिश रहती है,
हर ख़्वाब उससे,उसका अपना कहना बहुत है...
..
कबीर शब्दों-ग़ज़ल,वो ग़ज़ल मे डूब के रहती है,
नज़्म,गीत क्या लिखूं,वो मेरा ही हिस्सा लगती है...

Shubham Rajwanshi

Email : shubhamrajwanshi586@gmail.com

Instagram ID
Shubhamwriteups

तुम्हारा जिक्र मेरी कलम से..

कभी इजाजत तो कभी नकार देता है
हो जाए अगर बहुत गुस्सा तो मार देता है
वह अपनी तमाम ख्वाहिशें हंस के मार देता है
पिता जो तुम्हारी फिक्र में अपनी सारी उम्र गुजार देता है
पिता जो तेज धूप में छांव है
दर्द के समंदर में मरहम की नाव है
पिता जो रोजा के बाद निकला चांद है
हजारों दुखों को समेटे कोई बांध है
पिता दिन का खर्च रातों की मौज है
तुम्हारे पीछे खड़ी एक पूरी फौज है
पिता जो सारे घर का सुख है चैन है
सब जानकर भी रहता मौन है
पिता गर्म दिन में बारिश की फुहार है
घर की होली दिवाली सब त्यौहार है
जीवन की कड़वी सच्चाईयों ने भरा इतना ज्ञान है
पढ़ोगे तो जानोगे कि वह कितना महान है

तुम मिट्टी तो वह कुम्हार है
तुम कच्चे तो वह आग के समान है
कर उसके मुताबिक तुम पक जाओ
तो तुम्हारे जीवन में तरक्की अपार है

सेहत की फिक्र में तुम्हें बाहर का खाने नहीं देता
खाओ ना धोखा इसलिए ज्यादा दोस्त बनाने नहीं देता
तुम्हें कुछ हो ना जाए इस फिक्र में वह कायर
तुम्हें घर से दूर अकेले जाने नहीं देता

जब तक तुम घर नहीं लौटते वह रात भर जगता रहता है

तुम्हारे सब दुख दर्द तुम्हारे चेहरे से पढ़ लेता है
कहीं पीछे ना रह जाओ जमाने की दौड़ में
इसलिए दिल पर पत्थर रखकर तुम्हें घर से दूर जाने को कहता है

वह तुम्हारे खातिर तुम्हारी मां से लड़ जाता है
तुम्हारे जरा से पेट के दर्द से डर जाता है
तुम्हें जवान करते-करते वह पागल
जवान से बुद्धा फिर बीमार होकर मर जाता है

एक शाम तुम्हें घुमाना है भक्तिमय बनारस एक शाम तहजीब ए अवध
एक शाम गंगा आरती एक रोज रिवर फ्रंट की चमक
एक शाम बनारस हिंदू यूनिवर्सिटी एक शाम अवध विश्वविद्यालय की सड़क
एक शाम दशाश्वमेध घाट किनारे तैरती किश्तियां
एक शाम जनेश्वर पार्क में होती मस्तियां
एक शाम दिखाना है अस्सी घाट पर महादेव की आरतियां

एक शाम दिखाना है गोमती नगर में आजादी से घूमती लड़कियां
खान पान का अपना अलग अंदाज है
बनारस की चांट कचौड़ियां अवध के कवाब भी लाजवाब है
तुम थक ना जाना ना होना जरा भी सुस्त
लेंगे अस्सी घाट पर कचौड़ी चार्ट का मजा
उठाएंगे अमीनाबाद के टुंडे कबाब का भी लुफ्त
पिएंगे लंका की कुल्हड़ कॉफी और जी भर के लेंगे शर्मा के चाय की चुस्कियां
है तुम्हारी मर्जी तुम लेना प्रकाश खुल्फी मैं तो पियूंगा शिव भंडार की लस्सीयां

Megha Agarwal

She is from Jaipur. She is a mechanical Engineer and aspiring writer. She is currently working as freelancer content writer and digital marketer. *She is fire and ice.*

Email : megha3105agarwal@gmail.com
Instagram ID @banjaran_98

People Pleaser

I have seen people
People pleaser people
Always pleasing people
On the name of I am a Socially active person!
I have seen people
People-pleasing people to get fit in the group,
So they won't feel left out among people
As they Only care about If people like them or not
They want their spot in the community of famous people,
As they Think Famous people are Worthy then people with good intentions,
I have seen people
People pleaser People
Always pleasing people
They are licking the lies of the other people
They can't take stand as they are afraid of their position among So-called group of Four people
They are pleasing people at the cost of their belief as their
Belongingness among people is more than anything
I have seen people
People pleaser people
Always pleasing people
You will find people pleaser covering their insecurities from the
People among the people behind the people as they have no guts to
Standalone or Against the people
They are pleasing people
They are Promoting them to do wrong
They are the equal participants in the sin and good deeds of them
They are the one with No Belongingness
Even they are not bound to one particular community
These people pleaser are Homeless.

I have seen people,
People pleaser people,
Always pleasing people!

Aman Raj

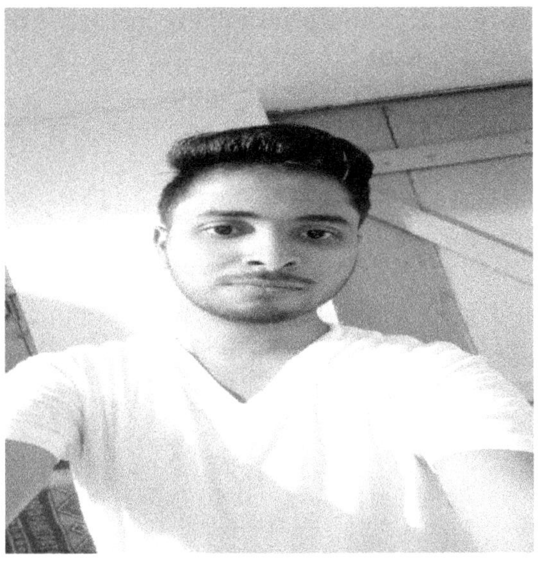

Aman Raj was born in Jamshedpur (Tata) and raised in Banka (Bihar). He is a 2nd year medical student in Jaipur (the pink city of Rajasthan). He dreams to became a best research scientist. And serve his mother India and being morals to it. He loves to study his favourite subject biology. He is also a motivational book reader. In his free time, he loves to draw and write such as poetry and inspirational story. He is also a deep thinker loves music to relax mind. He is also affection for the animals he loves to care for these and a enthiest in gardening of planting beautiful flowers.

Email : amanrajbanka123@gmail.com.
Instagram ID @am_an1680

Daddy

I know a pure soul full of care holding my hands and always be there with me, with me, with me, with me every time.
I know a face that always had a smile holding my hands and hiding his teary eyes every time, every time, every time, every time I can see.
How can I expect, it could be someone else because he knows me better, than anyone else and it's you, it's you, it's you, it's you dad.
Every time I see back in time, I always find him standing by my side holding my hands and supporting me ' n' times, in my failures, failures, failures
In my failures every time.
You killed your dreams.
Your passion changed the way of your fashion for me, for me, for me
For me every day.

And I don't know how much you love me all I know it's beyond infinity, I don't know how much I owe you but I guess it's more than my soul.
No matter how many times you have scolded me I remember every time you have moulded me with your love, with your care, with your strength, giving me more power to fight this cruel world. Every time when the school bells rang, I still remember having lunch from your hands as if it happened, it happened yesterday.
I don't remember when I called you dad but I know you have gone all mad.

When you heard me saying you first time dad, dad, dad and promise I'll never make you sad, I'll never make you sad.

And I'm not surprised you've known things before I could say!

I know a pure soul full of care holding my hands and always be there with me, with me, with me, with me every time.

And I don't know how much you love me all I know it's beyond infinity, I don't know how much I owe you but I guess it's more than my soul.

Sushmita Mishra

Myself Sushmita Mishra from Lucknow. I am a govt.teacher in Basic Education...Now lives in prayagraj.I am also a youtuber with multi skills like writing,dance,arts &crafts etc...

Email : mishrapreeti1505@gmail.com

Instagram ID
@kuch.to.logkaheng

ज़िन्दगी के रंग ...

मैं ज़िन्दगी के हर रंग को जीना चाहती हूँ
सिर्फ चमकदार बिना दाग वाला
सफेद पन्ना ही नहीं
बल्कि काला लाल पीला गुलाबी
हर रंग के सच से रूबरू होना चाहती हूँ
मैं ज़िन्दगी के हर ...
जैसे तितलियाँ उड़ती हैं ना
ढ़ेर सारे रंगों को एक साथ समेटे
बंद कली से खिले फूल तक
ठीक वैसे ही मैं भी हर उपवन में
फिरना चाहती हूँ..
लेकिन सिर्फ खिले फूलों की नहीं बल्कि
बेजान,मुरझाये फूलों की खुशबू भी
महसूस करना चाहती हूँ
मैं ज़िन्दगी के हर ...
जैसे चिड़ियाँ चहकती हैं,
दूर खुले आसमानों में,ठीक वैसे ही मैं भी
ढेर सारी ख्वाहिशों को अपने आँचल में समेटे.
बहुत दूर उस गगन में जाना चाहती हूँ
लेकिन सिर्फ खुले आसमान में ही नहीं
बल्कि जमीं पर बसी अनदिखी
संकरी गलियों से भी गुज़रना चाहती हूँ
मैं ज़िन्दगी के हर...
जैसे नदियाँ बहती हैं ना किसी कोने से
कल कल की धुन के साथ
वैसे ही मैं भी एकांत में रहना चाहती हूँ
लेकिन सिर्फ अपने ही मन की धुन नहीं
बल्कि ज़िन्दगी के हर सुर को सुनना चाहती हूँ...

मैं ज़िन्दगी के हर रंग ...
जैसे एक चित्रकार तस्वीर को
अपने मनचाहे रंगों से सजाता है ना...
ठीक वैसे ही मैं भी अपनी तस्वीर सजाना चाहती हूँ
लेकिन सिर्फ अपनी पसंद के रंगों से नहीं
बिना भेदभाव के दुनिया के हर रंग से
उसको रंगना चाहती हूँ
मैं जिंदगी के हर रंग को जीना चाहती हूँ...

Bhavik Pathak

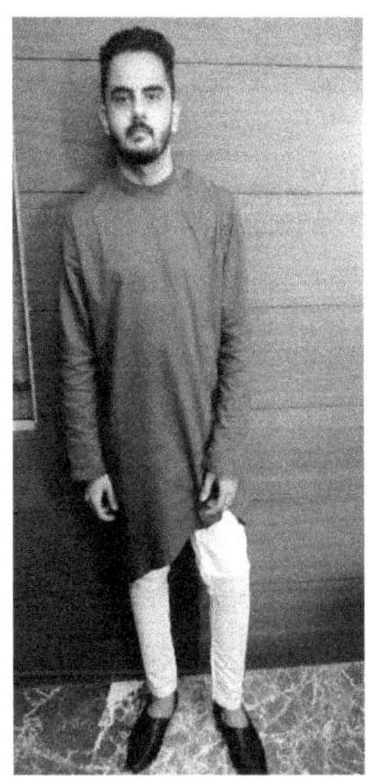

Bhavik Pathak, he is from Rajkot Gujarat. He is marketing manager for e commerce company and has own business and a freelance content writer. He loves to write and he also counsel person who are facing depression. He wants to write so that people around the world can relate and feels that they are not alone.

Email:- bhavikpathak769@gmail.com.

Instagram ID: @bhavik_93

Just A Touch

just a touch of your fingers
can restart flow of my blood,
your hand on my hand
and i can defeat this world,
just a hug can provide me a hope,
a purpose to relive,
even your fake smile can get me
our of this ongoing battle,
a kiss can regenerate my soul
just a glance and volcanoes
erupt in my veins
you can make my bygones disappear,
you can channelize my emotions
into single ball of emotion which
reminds me of my only purpose
that is to be part of your soul,
because of you I am
well-coordinated with my life
without you I am a shadowy presence
your farewells make me achingly sad,
just carry me close with you
because its hard to invest emotionally
when I cannot feel your presence

Secrets

Some chapters of your life are
never meant to be published,
either you live with them alone
or you just skip that chapter,
but if you relive
you live it with your grief
in your dimension,
no one should exist between
you and your chapter,
you read that chapter
and keep it for yourself
its meant to be that way
till the grave

Shubham Tyagi

Shubham Tyagi,29 years old from Punjab, India. He is an outspoken personality with an optimistic outlook to worldly life. A choreographer who is also the director of ONE STEP AHEAD DANCE STUDIO. He is a vice president of Punjab under DANCE Federation of INDIA.

He is a creative person who loves to write and draw. He used to write those moment from which he has passed or he is going through or on the situation of his surroundings. He has worked in more than 25 Anthology books.

Email : dancestudioonestepahead@gmail.com

Follow him on Instagram page :

@shubhamtyagi_osa

@haqikat_e_bayan

Just That Is The Question!

Sure, on the truth so,
But I doubt on what I sure
your every word is true,
Is it true or is not!
Just that is the question
And the answer to this question is
Also, a question in itself....

The question is only on one matter
Which you use to tell me and I use to notice
And i noticed that you used to say me
That you love me a lot.
Was that love or is not!
Just that is the question
And the answer to this question is
Also, a question in itself....

You said that you are in me
If you are in me then, where are you?
I ask you to be with me you left that to.
Thou you are near to me or far away
I actually don't know
Just that is the question
And the answer to this question is
Also, a question in itself....

Nothing much i asked you
I just ask you for one demanded
Why you failed to give me love
In exchange of my trust.
Today where you left me
Tomorrow will he also be the same
Just that is the question
And the answer to this question is
Also, a question in itself....

Did you still remember that moments?
Which we spend together
That first kiss, my first gift
And the night outs which we went together
I stand right there today also
But you're not there with me
I pray god to keep u happy
Maybe we can meet again?
Will we meet or not!
Just that is the question
And the answer to this question is
Also, a question in itself....

Bheemparam Kishore Kumar

Bheemparam Kishore Kumar,
Even though by profession is a Medico at Kakatiya Medical College, Warangal. he is one among the passionate writer comming up with his talent fresh words. The way he frames his lines perfectly go in sync with the content. He has worked as Co-author for 5 anthologies.
He is always thankful to his friends & family as they in each step supported in writing in improving himself.
"He believes the art of saving lives inspires in making art of everything he can. When you feel the things happening around you, every word you speak can be made an art of it."

1) The day he realized,
Traveling with her isn't the drug for his disturbed state of mind,
but travelling itself a drug...
His Life took a turn to make himself a Happy soul.

2) The maroon lipstick on her lips,
Black dress wrapped around her soul…
Holding her troubles, waiting for his soul
For the thing just to show him...
How his thoughts & words were reflecting in her beauty.

3) She was the one writing our love story…
& Me was just narrating the tale Myself.

4) her lips dance for his lips singing… but the irony stands here both singing and dancing does together kissing each other

5) He then realized why his lips starts to taste, the flavour of Dark chocolate after kissing her.

6) I think we need to have more life together, in the bottle of wine drowning together in trance. Making the unhappened things happen.

7) If beauty has a life for sure it would be jealous of You. the way the edge of your hair curled... the complete smile…. beautifully expressive Eyes… calmness in her soul. finally realized her beauty could never be explained in words.

8) 10 years after their breakup… he could still feel her walk inside him.

Salyali Das

She is Salyali Das, the young enthusiastic & dynamic lady who follows her dreams and loves her passion. She is born and brought up in Kolkata, a pure bong lady. She is a published author beside being a manager of a company... She is participant of 25+ anthologies as co-author, now she is also compiling her own anthologies.

To connect her email her at

salyalidas@gmail.com

To know her thoughts better, have a look & follow her on her Instagram profile : @salyalidas

Love In Boundary

She is bound in a boundary,
Where limitations get the priority
And the love comes in secondary...!
Neither she has the right to speak,
Nor by own anything to decide;
Being limitless once she was being known,
But now she is living in the captivity,
Everything being told to her; she now just has to abide...!

Every evening while he comes back home from office,
Seeing him she misses her earlier daily life;
But who cares! No-one even bothers to ask,
If she wants these pages from her life, just to swipe…!

The love he gave,
The care he took,
The concern he showed;
Getting those she was once being flowed...!
The limitations he gave, to those the concern he named;
Taking the decision to be with him,
To herself she is now being blamed!
No-one to share her sorrows now,

She has lost her inner smile;
Still she fears,
That the love might get drained completely, just in a while…!
But he is happy,
Unaware of the fact, from inside how much she is getting fragile!
Love in a boundary is painful,
Yet is a bliss to her though awhile...!

Rhythm Gandhi

Rhythm is a writer . Writing for every cause is her passion. Giving the limelight to the topics which no one takes seriously is actually her true aim. She gives her best in providing the write-ups that everyone could read and also make the difference after the impact of it. The aim is to be a bold journalist and this is just the start up for her career and future.

1)
The hidden corner of my heart wants to fly high in the sky. I never want to stop, just want to move forward in life. I want to be a person with no limitations and boundaries. I want to be away from all the chores here on the land and fly high and high.

2)
Im not a person running away from my problems but its just I want to rediscover my strengths and the only way is flying high and high in the sky and even above that. Because I have always heard that in silence we get our best answers. And out there, silence and calmness rests.

3)
For me I can just relate this topic more relevantly with a woman's life. How she wants to fly high in the sky with a hope in her eye. She has dreams in her heart which is normally suppressed by the other people which lately is a part inside her heart which wants to fly away from every situation and be happy for who she is.

4)
The hidden corner of her heart is talented and skillful just the way she is so blissful. There always a dexterous girl in every woman's heart that want to fly high in the sky. Where no one is seeing her flaws and judging her. She wants to escape just because she doesn't get the worth that cost millions if we really and truly see the broken and the unsaid part inside her heart.

5)
The part she is taking along since the first time she was stopped to fly in the sky with her success. Not only her future but also her desires and hopes are killed when she is stopped from living a dignified life by touching the sky. Yes, sky that's what her dream is but never accomplished. that's her reach where she was never able to reach because of various reasons.

6)
She might seem happy outside but that little hidden corner of her still wants to fly high and high, away where she can be qualified, never stop her from flying if you don't want that little dark hidden corner of heart.

7)- a girl who wants to fly high and high.

Nishigandha Das

A mathematician in the making, dreams of becoming an entrepreneur and remove unemployment. Loves traveling and exploring new places and cuisines and also fond of photography.

E-mail: nishigandhadas5@gmail.com

Broke…

People say that life often gives us lemonade. But in my life that lemonade hasn't arrived that often. I was having a normal life like any other girl in this world. But two years ago, everything changed. It was the time when my boyfriend broke up with me. I was devastated. So devastated that I called up my ex-boyfriend and started hanging out with him. One day I went to his place to party and eventually I got horribly drunk there. I lost control over myself. My ex-boyfriend took advantage of this situation and took me to his bedroom, locked the door and switched off the lights. He lay near me on the bed and started touching me in an uncomfortable way. He then slid his hand under my top, unhooked my bra and started touching my breasts. Then he slowly unzipped my pants and put his hand under my panty. I tried to stop him from doing this but I couldn't. I was drunk and had very less energy in my body to stop him. He almost raped me. This incident broke me from inside. I was ashamed as well as angry upon myself. I regret that I couldn't do anything that day. I had nobody to share all these things. Not because I had no friends, but because we are Indians. We Indians assume things on our own without listening to the whole story and as always blame the girl. Nobody will look at the sick mentality of the guy. People will blame the girl's parents and question them their upbringing. But nobody will question the guy and his parents and will never ask them from where they got this mentality.

This is today's society. We all have smart phones in our pockets, have high qualification and jobs but still have the narrow-minded thinking whenever it comes to cases like rape.

GUARANGI SINGH

Hope within eyes and sky as a limit, with a mixture of bubbly and bold character figuring and exploring ways to hone herself the future HR department head, Gaurangi Singh. Pursuing BCom from esteemed Delhi University for whom writing is what that keeps her sane! Strongly having a belief "Treat the people the way u wants to be treated" Having a zest to live the life to the fullest! Writing has always been a way to express herself when she has no words! In this chaotic and deceptive world where nothing is true and everything comes for a price, writing is what that assures her that still, she can hope for Rainbows in dark valleys!!

Will I Ever Be Me??

Looking at the blank pages speaking
Stories to me that are never heard.
I think to myself is this is what
Has come in the end!
Feeling a gut reaching pain of grief
Yet still smiling like nothing ever
Made me weep!
Am I being myself?
Looking at the astounding nature,
That gives me hope and tells me
That yes, I am here for you.
But is u ever really there!?
I am hopping like a bumblebee
Searching for the nectar that heals me
Nourishes me, strengthens me!!
Am I being too selfish??
For all the uncountable days that
I grief is it too much to ask for?
I fear will I ever be me?
But then I smell the scent of rain
That guides me that you are everything
That you wish to be!!
The sun embraces me with its magic
And tells me the nectar is you, my dear.
The calm in the wind that soothes
My Strom from within and gives
Me the everlasting peace I craved for!
“Yes, you will be you,” it says.
I am the circum-horizon in the sky
Of dark!
The Juliet rose of my garden and
Yes, I will try that I am me!

For miracles happen in a day and
No stars fall every day!
It's all about finding me
I guess I can be the real "Me"

This Is What It Comes To In End!

Walking on the pathway to chisel,
Myself into perfection,
Yet again pausing to see the beauty,
Of roses bud that guides my way.
Circumhorizons beaming the sparkle,
Of my eyes,
For all I know is That what
I look for in my way.
Happy go soul, beaming with hope,
To soar the heights.
Taking sky as a limit
For this is everything I could ever wish for,
But then hit by the sudden
The chaos of my feelings,
Pushing me to verge of insanity,
In my defence for I allow myself to,
Understand this vividly,
But nothing seems to work
Is this my fault?

Snehasish Kanungo

Snehasish is currently working as an ASM in Voltas Limited, Jamshedpur. He has pursued his PGDM from BIMTECH, Noida in Marketing stream. Apart from his professional life, he is passionate towards writing, playing tabla & collecting coins. He has also been awarded with the Best Tabla Player award during his academic year.

Poverty- Manifestation of Deterioration

Thoughts of development have gained priority,
Without incomes of rural & urban households having relished parity ;
Ages will come & go still the Thoughts cannot be honoured Until,
The matured minds act towards slackening the basic cause i.e. Poverty…

The term has often been referred yet the depth has never been understood,
Ideas have been developed to assist yet less profitable ventures have always been overlooked;
The torments of destitute are enigmatic while touring the backward areas within closed panes
Because,
The profundity cannot be perceived until confronted with the poverty-stricken livelihood …

The underprivileged population constitutes this democratic country's Majority;
Leave alone democracy, they suffer the most in obtaining basic amenity;
It is the deprived who maintains the cleanliness of the surroundings
However,
Even their residential areas have been classified as Slums & Austere society…
Having bestowed with nourishment resulting from a farmer's toil;
Respect granted is much less than deserved by that worshipper of the soil;

The money he fetches confirms of his unacknowledged sheer efforts
As,

Unable to repay loans, suicide becomes facile amid the aroused turmoil…

Likewise, tenderness of palms ceases in shaping a house to perfection;
While the radiating sun would have the labourers panting with exertion;
With construction, Fondness of residing within four walls of own grows
Yet,
Dearth income compels many to slumber under naked sky slaying their pr edilection…

With compulsion of reservation for the indigent;
In addition, schemes of equal income opportunity to ease their torment;
Not only the slow poison to progress be sedated
But Also,
The masses can count upon their Nation's Bona fide achievement…

Rutuja Pardeshi

Rutuja is an 18 year old with a messy mind and little heart. She is a content head and finds her comfort in words and philosophy. Cold nights, stars and coffee makes her pen down her feelings. She has control issues so things are always in check around her. All she is looking for is love and adventures.

Email:- rutujapardeshi7@gmail.com
Instagram ID:- luv_rutu

The Agony Of A Breaking Heart

They say, when your heart breaks, your heart takes far longer to accept the reality than your brain. And I guess that is why after a break up your brain is in a constant war with your heart. If you are anything like me, you would wait for them to come back, or find a reason to go back; maybe he didn't mean it, maybe it was his anger speaking not him. And the other moment you would be hating yourself for loving him.

This constant state of dilemma continues all day long. You miss them in the lyrics of the song you bonded over, you miss them in the morning coffee you both had together. Everything around you seem to make you feel the emptiness you now have. For the good riddance of those evocations you decide to keep yourself busy and get to work. The popping wallpaper on your laptop doesn't help you either and instead of work files you shift your cursor to memories. You open the folder that's most dangerous for you and yet you don't stop yourself. You start going through every photo, getting your heart nailed with a hammer with each passing photo from the folder. All the rush of emotions makes you select the entire folder so that you can delete it within seconds but just seconds before clicking on it, you get this ache in your heart and you push away the laptop. You just sit there breathing slowly and silently, comparing the pain of just losing his pictures to actually losing him.

With every passing moment it gets harder and harder to stay home. The walls of your room start echoing his voice and his words, leaving you with no choice but to go out. You get in the car and drive as far as possible. A million of emotions and thoughts run through your mind, all you can see is a clear road with his voice still echoing in your ears. Suddenly you stop and you get out of the car and realize that the road down the memory lane brought you to the same place with a thousand memories you once shared. You curse yourself for even opening the folder and for every memory you have of that led you to this emptiness. You see the sun setting down and the birds flying all around in hurdles in the reddish-orange colored sky. With every crumb of sun going down you want to scream on

the highest note of your voice hoping that cry would reach him. But with all the weight of emotions over your little heart, all you do is silently shed tears under the open sky. As you see the reddish-orange sky turn into cotton candy pink color and later into dark blue black one filled with infinite twinkling stars, you pull yourself together and get in the car and drive back home with one sad song on loop. You have heard this song a lot of times earlier but this time it hits you differently, you feel every word of the song and you live with every line in it.

You stop in your parking lot, staring into darkness hoping to disappear in it. Trapped in the circle of reality, you get back to your empty apartment. This time you give up, you give up fighting against that gut instinct in yourself and let it all out. You cry from every inch of your body and dry out as much as tears one possibly could. Your heart screams his name with all the pain in your heart, begging the universe to reverse the time and make it alright. You wish to have one more moment of relief, one more moment of happiness, one more moment of laughter, one more moment of comfort, one more moment of love with him in a hope that if you kept adding 'one mores" it would equal a lifetime.

With all this clogging your mind and heart you put yourself to sleep. And wake up the next morning with the thought of him not being around and the feeling of emptiness within you even before you open your eyes.

As I was finishing writing this, he entered the room with a bright smile and I put all these thoughts in a corner of my heart. All these years I learned to live my pain through my words under the name of fiction writings, hiding the deepest-darkest emotions leaving a hole in my heart, burying all those past memories under the tons of happiness he gives me, trying to fill the void that was once created.

Upasana Borbora

21-year-old, starving hard to express and feel essence of life.
Herself Upasana Borbora
A student of B.sc(Nursing), indeed working out for small pleasures in life with respect to serving mankind at its best.
A resident of Guwahati, Assam.

Desires

When she blushes and whisper his name to be hers again,The stars smile!
As if they are the one who would let him know the love of theirs and how she isn't over it yet.
The stars ask do they even need to shine?
Or dull up seeking for his replies! You got her right?
How would you neither not know? Fuck such dilemmas.
She loves yes, she loves
Getting back past memories of how the mirror knew, how standing right again would bring a different glow in a different way, But still she chooses to be simple and his favourite.
How holding hands shivers hands and legs,How kissing beats up heart fast,
And how loving makes more in them to love!
But these are closed once again on pages of diaries wrapped in colours of love and shining bright as the rainbow with smiling colours
Hatred~Let the chaos created redefine her in a verge of realistic awe
To the one gazing sunsets, indeed an opposite of one loving dark sky with the twinkling stars attracts all of her attention!
Nobody could ruin her evenings and nobody dared too.
Hoping, the jealous moon could never see her catching eyeblinks with the stars, talking once again about love
One whose smile took all of her breath for a second, to the one whose presence mattered to enjoy life with bliss, never allowed heart to stop racing

Dilemmas

A thousand of reason to smile,
Yet millions of reasons to be sad!
Just as we choose greater numbers, emotions also sometimes prefer to set priorities maybe?
Ain't that silly to hear?
Of course yes, yet no.
Dilemma once sucking through veins deeply!
~ Common form of human

Tears~Just as heavy clouds drop down tears of droplets and mesmerizes the ground spreading fragrance of sorrows, My tears of love spreads fragrance of my favourite person around, Holding back to evenings of satisfaction and talking about a planned future, somewhere in between , we knew we would never be apart. But we were wrong for this time, life had prepared another heartbreak for us This was what we were meant to hold today, sharing words through writings, and giving back replies where both knew was for one another You know better, best
Take a breath,~With alternate vibes and lapse of time, once again reminiscing memories. But this evening, I got more to love ,rather than tearing pages of diaries and telling once again" I LOVE YOU" Cause you taught me better things to love then just saying it.
Can you ans~I often question, what was wrong with us? What was wrong in our love? How could we give up so easily? How could we not fight back for our love? How could our egos, our angers, win over our love? Love which was lost was found again, didn't we promised to say forever? What was wrong in you and me? Why did we listen to others? Why did we not talk ourselves? Why did we leave empty everything so easily? Was our love not perfect? Was our love so greedy ? Was our love so cruel and mean? I wish, I could get you ! I wish I could love again. I wish I could change us I wish you could just erase out hatreds. All I wish is, I wish and wish to love back.

Ekta Singh

She is Ekta Singh. She has been working as a co-author in several books, she wants to upgrade herself at different platforms in life.

Love For Happiness

In the search of happiness,
Instead to be happy,
We have started worrying about the happiness.
Happiness is not something that's Lost in the universe.
It's inside us,
We need to remove the bandages
Of worry!

To feel the happiness.
From being worried faces,
Be a relaxed face.
Being anxious in nature will
Bring you down, be carefree.
Love the beauty indeed your heart
Embrace the love.

Kumari Tripti

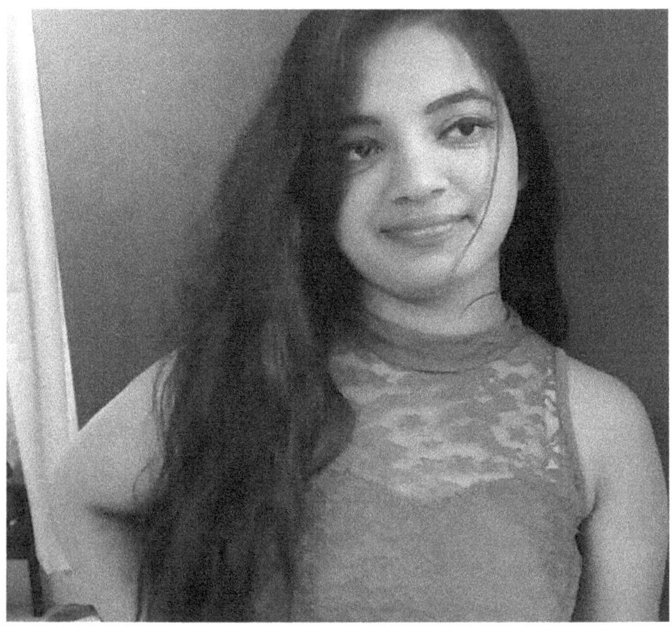

Tripti is a curious girl who believes that's hard work and determination can help her achieve all her goals. Despite battling with her health for almost her entire life she was resilient in making her dreams come true. She loves writing, and had been publishing her works such as stories, poetries and shayaris on international platforms.

Kindred Soul

We share secrets, we laugh and even cry...
We have so much in common, good
Concerns, likes and dislikes.

Ours is a relationship joined by Tender velvet chains that link
our similar dreams of life and love.

A gentle intuition guides us in our individual struggles to
succeed at the things we pursue,
To stand out from the crowd.

In you I have found so much of myself,
Including many of the same insecurities and philosophy.

Complete inner-peace and happiness,
These are the things I wish for you,
In the present and in the future because you are my kindred
soul.

Find Your Inner Wings

I always wanted to fly like a bird.
Be like a bird.
I'd go to places I've never been before,
O... How wonderful it would be!
I always wondered I could escape my problems,
That flying away from them would be the only solution.
I could just be free, strong and careful,
Not a single worry in the world.
I world I knew would change, oh how desperately I want to fly....
I prayed to God to give me wings, until I realised myself,
I already had them; I just wasn't ready to face my worries.
I just wasn't ready to be strong and accept them

Arshi Gupta

A MBA HR by Profession, a writer by hobby and choice, hails from Rampur, Uttar Pradesh. Post Graduate from Chandigarh University in Human Resource (HR) and Finance. She started writing from 18th February 2019 via YourQuote App, she used to write Motivational Quotes over there so that she can influence people and they can relate it from their life and can be motivated. When she initially started writing after few quotes she starts receiving appreciation which motivates her to forward her understanding and sense of thought to more people. Her key competencies are Leadership qualities and Self-reliant nature. She does have a belief that no one can beat you until and unless we don't start losing or settling down for less. Her aim is to publish her own book soon in the market, so that her voice and thoughts can be heard to more and more people and her words can receive love and positive response from the audience.

The Hidden Corner Of My Heart

In today's scenario we often heard people talking about their incomplete stories, failures, struggles, depression, hard times they have been fighting with, Why do people do all this? What makes people so helpless they have to face these challenges, answer is pretty simple, "Their Dreams", dream to be successful, to reach to a height where everything looks so affordable, and to be someone from where you may see people following you and admiring you at their best.

This is the sweetest thing each and every youth is hiding in their corner of the heart, they know the path is difficult, they are stuck among the directions, but they will get through this and will be satisfied one or the another day in life.

Well apart from this, there are some cute 1sided love stories as well which many people hide in the corner of the heart just because they know it might be able to affect their current relations with their dearest one's.

The Heart also holds some secrets, secret of fear, secret of losing someone, secret of betrayal, secret of violence, secret of memories, secret of love and happiness.

Secret of fear comes up with the harsh and bad memories made in childhood,

Secret of Losing Someone comes up with the first breakup in teenager's life,

Secret of Betrayal comes up with those friends and family who betrays you for fulfilling their own desires and needs,

Secret of Violence comes up with those people who are extraordinary dominating and controlling, who feels themselves as the most Superior One's among all of the people,

Secret of Memories comes up with all the bad and good moments which we visualize on our own, although some predictions are never meant to be ascertained but if those

imaginations can bring some temporary smile on our face then it is really good to imagine,
Secret of Love comes up with all our different relations, whether it is with our sibling, parents, cousins, friends, best friends, relatives or with some random casual person, each one of us holds some special relation of love, affection and care.
Please ensure that it's not our heart which makes us store all these kinda feelings but it's us who make our heart burden with these mixtures of feelings.

"IT NEVER MEANT TO KEEP SOMEONE ON HOLD, BROKEN OR STEP BACK FOR A WHILE, BUT YOUR DREAMS MAKE YOU TO DO THAT"..!!
When once we burden our heart with so different kinda emotions, we started complaining and creating mess in life, it's not like we can never compile our two or three dreams at a time but to achieve this we start lacking in our daily required necessities, we think that if we be left alone in a room we can focus for long hours but it never happened like that, we even start doing those imaginations which is surely not going to be possible any day, then what is the use of keeping ourselves away from the real and actual life, this is true, this is the real and real secret which most people hide in their corners of the heart, I believe that instead of making distance, build more and more communications with those who are nearby to you, possibly then we can get some better ideas or suggestions which may make us one step closure to our dreams.
Most Importantly, sometimes we do hurt someone's emotions or keep someone hold for our own dreams or benefits, if one day we anyhow able to reach to our dreams but then won't be able to achieve or retain it for longer, for sure, keep this as a secret inside the corners of the heart.

Ayush Saxena

Hey! My name is Ayush Saxena. I'm an engineer with profession but A writer with passion. You could listen my poetry on YouTube(MERA DARD). Or search on google just write down- "*chot khayi hai apno se hmne*".

Email : ayushsaxena198@gmail.com
Insta id- er_ayush_saxena

अचानक डर सा गया...

खुशियो से भरा मन अचानक डर सा गया,
पल यूं गुजरे, जैसे धूप से बादल छट सा गया...
बचपन की बातें याद आयी ..
खुशियों से भरा मन अचानक डर सा गया....
ये सोच मेरा दिल उदासी से भर गया. .
वो वेपरवाह जिंदादिल कहा खो गया ,
अभी तो मेरा बचपन था,
इतनी जल्दी कैसे बड़ा हो गया,
खुशियों से भरा मन अचानक डर सा गया ....
बचपन मे चला था पतंग से आकाश नापने-2
मांझा कहीं धूप में झुलस गया,
खुशियों से भरा मन अचानक डर सा गया .....
क्या दिन थे वो , क्या थी रातें
ना कोई डर था , ना चिंता की बातें ,
वो हंसना वो खेलना सब छूट सा गया...
खुशियों से भरा मन अचानक डर सा गया...
बचपन के सारे सपने चकनाचूर हो गए,
घर से निकलते ही हम सबसे दूर हो गए,
जीवन की मजबूरियों मे कहीं दब सा गया,
खुशियों से भरा मन अचानक डर सा गया....

Lockdown

इंसान कितना मजबूर हो गया.....
एक वायरस के चक्कर मे,
अपने ही घरों मे कैद हो गया,
इंसान कितना मजबूर हो गया......
मज़दूर बेटा,
पैदल ही चल पड़ा गांव के लिए-2,
सड़क पर वो भूखा ही मर गया,
इंसान कितना मजबूर हो गया....
घर तक ना पहुंच सका लॉकडाउन में,
एक बेटा माँ से हमेशा के लिए दूर हो गया,
इंसान कितना मजबूर हो गया.....
किसी की शादी की खुशी,
किसी की मौत का ग़म,
आना- जाना सब बंद हो गया,
इंसान कितना मजबूर हो गया,
अपने ही घरों मे कैद हो गया ।

Dhivya Bharathi Arumugasamy

Diya, born on 24th June 1999, is a medical student and an aspiring writer from the southern state, TamilNadu, India. She spent most of her childhood days in her native until she went abroad for her higher education. She loves to travel. When not writing, she loves listening music and is a tea lover. she is a bibliophile. She used to do things that makes her happy.

Email : b.dhiviya@yahoo.com
Instagram @_b.l.a.c.k_d.a.i.r.y , @dhivya_diya

I Lost Myself In Search Of Him

It's getting colder, the sun hid her amidst the clouds, the chillness of the air, the mist and the foggy air all started with a cup of tea. I never thought it would be my special day that i got lost myself at the sight of him. It's one of those strange feelings that I've ever had in my entire life. I wish I could explain his eyes how beautiful it is, how the sound of his voice gives me butterflies, and how his smile makes my heart skip a beat. I want him to be my cup of tea and I wish I could see him every morning as I wake up. And I wanna hold his hands for a walk amid the city streets. Forever is a long time but I wouldn't mind spending by his side. Is this passion? Is this obsession? Is this madness? Or is this just craziness?

"The truth is I'm crazy about you and everyone can see it, except you"

The More You Hide Your Feelings For Someone, The More You Fall For Them.

I never thought I'd like someone this much and never thought of having someone on my mind this often. And yes I think about him a little more than I should. I never thought I could be so obsessed until I met him. I tend to lose myself whenever I look into his eyes. There is nothing about him that I don't adore. I wish there is no escape between him and me. I'm afraid to lose him even though he is not mine to lose. I chose him, I'll choose him and within a heartbeat I'll keep choosing him, but my biggest fear is his NO.

"To be loved by someone is ok but to love someone unconditionally without expecting love in return is a kind of feeling that one cannot expresses by words"

Qaima Hussain

My_ limit? Infinity
Qaima:).
-solitary
-liberated
-curative
-shayri page:)@yaadgarein_Zindagi
From heaven to earth
You_sure_you_wana_play_with_the_fire.
Email : qaimahussain11@gmail.com

-My Virtual Pen-

Manzilein bhi uski thi
Arman bhi uska tha
Ek mai akela tha
Kafila bhi uska tha
Sath sath chlne ki soch
bhi uski thi
Dur jane ka faisla
bhi uska tha
Aaj kyu preshan hu?
Dil sawal krta hai
Log to uske the,
Kya khuda bhi uska tha....!
Yaadgarein_Zindagi

Adiba

Adiba is completed her Mcom and D.el.ed
She is preparing for C.Tet as well as Banking
And have interest in reading.
Email : adibakhalid1997@gmail.com

Andhuri Mohabbat

Kya likho ab tere bare me..
Haa ab kya likho tere bare me..
Tere mohabbat ka junoon itna…
Ha teri mohabbat ka junoon itna
Ki 101ayama saas ke saath caha tujhe…
Tu mera woh khayal hai jisko maine bekhayali me bhi socha…
Ha ab kya likho mai tere bare me…
Tu meri zindagi ka woh hissaa jisko mai caho bhi to nahi mita sakti
Ha 101ayamat woh khayal jisko maine bekhayali me bhi socha..
Tu jab lautega raah e mohabbat me bht der ho chuki hogi
Deewani teri patjhad ke patto si bikhar chuki hogi Intezaar tera rahega jab tak aakhri 101ayamat ki ghadi hogi Dunya lut chuki hogi par ye isi dorahe pe pagli khadi hogi…

Ek Tarfa

Ab kya likhu tere bare me..
haa ab likhu mai tere bare me ..
Tum meri woh mohabbat ho jisme fasle na ho kr bhi milo ke fasle
Maine to tujhe apni har saas ke sath caha lekin sayad tune mujhe kabhi nahi caha tune mujhe kabhi nahi caha Ha teri zindagi me meri kabhi woh ahmiyat nahi jiski mai haqdar ho par ab mohabbat ek tarfa hi sahi Tu bolta hai waqt nahi mere pass
Par Asal baat to ye hai ki tujhe dena hi nahi woh waqt mujhe
Ha ab nahi tera intizar nahi cahiye tera waqt kabhi priority(talab) bani hi nahi mai teri... Ha ab kya likho tere bare me tujhe to maine bekhayali me bhi socha ha Teri har ek adat par mai ho marti
Ha teri har ek ada par mai ho marti
Tujhe nahi ho cahati mai khona kabhi
Par ye ek tarfa mohabbat kab dam tod de kya pata
Par maine to bekhayali me bhi tujhe hi socha hai

Rita Kakkar

I am e retied head of a govt high school rajpura.. Punjab.. Distt patiala... I am the owner of ankur memorial trust. Under this i give food plate for rupess 10 to the needy people and give clothes for rupees 10 to the needy people... I am a social worker also. I am a writer.my poems are published in many local newspapers and in magzines... My poems are published in shabdoo ka karrva book just few days back...

Email : ritadardhidard@gmail.com

आखरी उम्मीद

यह रात...... यह तन्हाई......
यह दिल के धड़कने की आवाज
और यह सन्नाटा.......
यह डूबते हुए तारों की खामोश ग़ज़ल जैसी आवाज......
यह वक्त की पलकों पर सोई हुई वीरानी.........
जज्बाते मोहब्बत की यह आखरी अंगड़ाई.....
शायद मौत की शहनाई.....
आ तुझे बुलाती हूँ सिर्फ कुछ पल के लिए आ जा.....
बंद होती हुई मेरी आंखों में एक राहत का ख्वाब सजा जा......

तकाजा

यह कह रही है तुझे छूकर आने वाली हवा.....
उदास में ही नहीं बेकरार तू भी है
मेरी उदासियों को कहीं तू यह ना समझ लेना....
कि तेरे प्यार को मायूस कर रही हूं मैं....
वह उम्मीद जो तेरी आंखों में जगमगाई थी.. .
अब वह दूर से महसूस कर रही हूं मैं....
कैसे बताऊं कि तेरीआरजू भी है....
पर अभी तो मुझे हालात का तकाजा है...
कि दूर रहकर भी मैं प्यार को निभाती हूं.. ...
शिकन ना आए कभी जिंदगी के माथे पर.....
दिल पर चोट लगे मगर फिर भी मुस्कुराती हूँ.....
शायद इसी में हमारी मोहब्बत की आबरू है.....
यह कह रही है तुझे तू के आने वाली हवा...
के उदास में ही नहीं बेकरार तू भी है.....

जिंदगी एक चिता

लगता है जिंदगी एक सुलगती हुई चिता है...
और मै इसे सिसक सिसक कर गुजार रही हूं ....
मैं बहुत कोशिश कर रही हूं कि....
धुंधली पड़ चुकी लाशों में से जिंदगी की उम्मीद ना करूं....
मगर क्या करूं तेरे एहसास का नशा मुझे भूलता ही नहीं.....
तेरा अकश मेरी आंखों में तैरता रहता है.....
और फिर एक सुलगता अक्श नमी बन कर मेरी आंखों में उभरता है....
मैं बेबस सा हो के उस अख्स को आसूँ बनने से रोकती हूं.....
फिर चौक उठती हूं मैं और देखती हूं कि तुम तो एक तस्वीर में हो वैसे ही जैसे बहुत साल पहले थे....

Anamika Tiwari

Anamika Tiwari was born on 1st December 1995. She is always fluent with words and has always a taste of rhymes in her conversation. She has recently completed her higher studies. Although, She was not always a studios girl but when it comes to poetry she always put a mark on people's heart with her simple language and culture to explain love or what it is to love be in love in today's life. She has started her journey in poetry just like every other poet, with a dairy and a pen and then deciding it to posting on page through social networking site. And now she is been receiving so much of love.

Email : kabirpankaj92@gmail.com
Instagram ID:- @laaf_

रिश्ते

हसी के पीछे के गम को देख
आंखो के चमक के पीछे आसुं देख
आजादी के पीछे उसकी बंदिश देख
अगर तू प्यार करता है तो कह कर देख
मास के टुकड़े के लिए वो जिस्म मत देख
ओरत के साथ साथ उसका दिल देख
तवायफ है तो क्या हुआ
प्यार करने का हक देकर तो देख
प्यार करने का हक उनको भी ह
उनका प्यार आजमा कर तो देख
उजाले म दखकर चार बार नहाते है रात म वहीं जाकर मुंह मारते ह
रात में नहीं दिन मै अपना के देख
अधिकारी को अधिकार केह के देख
घरवाली को घरवाली कह के देख
तवायफ को तवायफ कह के देख
तू डरेगा तू झिझकेगा पर तू तवायफ नहीं कह के देखेगा
इज्जत लेकर नहीं इज्जत देकर दख
वो किसी की बेटी है, बीवी है, मा है, सेहली है
पर तेरे आगे वह कोठी की तवायफ दखती है
तू कोई रिश्ता निभा के देख
वो हर रिश्ते निभाने म माहिर होती हैस्म मत देख
तवायफ है तो क्या हुआ
प्यार करने का हक देकर तो देख
प्यार करने का हक उनको भी है
उनका प्यार आजमा कर तो देख
उजाले में देखकर चार बार नहाते है रात में वहीं जाकर मुंह मारते हैं
रात में नहीं दिन में अपना के देख
अधिकारी को अधिकार केह के देख

घरवाली को घरवाली कह के देख
तवायफ को तवायफ कह के देख
तू डरेगा तू झिझकेगा पर तू तवायफ नहीं कह के देखेगा
इज्जत लेकर नहीं इज्जत देकर देख
वो किसी की बेटी है, बीवी है, माँ है, सेहली है
पर तेरे आगे वह कोठी की तवायफ दखती है
तू कोई रिश्ता निभा के देख
वो हर रिश्ते निभाने म माहिर होती है

King Idr

Inder Jeet Singh (born 21 November 1993), better known by his pen name King Idr is an Indian Sikh writer, singer, song writer, rap writer, poet and shyer. He was born in Meerut, Uttar Pradesh on 21 November 1993. His father (Late. Kundan Singh) belonged to Khadoor Sahib, Distt. Tarn Taran, Punjab was a truck driver who died when he was of 3 years old. King's mother (Sarabjeet Kaur) is a very struggling and brave lady. Who struggled much to educate both of her sons (King Idr & Simran Jeet Singh known as Rap Badshah Royal Jatt). Due to the problems King was well known about everything from his childhood like he never feels childhood. He started writing from a teenage but later he started to keep writing on his notebook and as he became young. King started to share his own quotes with people on social media.

Email : ijsingh.singh75@gmail.com
Instagram ID
https://www.instagram.com/kingidr/

*" किसी के कहने पर एक दिन घमंड की जगह सांसें ले ली
उसी दिन से तबियत खराब है मेरी"* - KING IDR

" दिन रोज़ आता है रात रोज़ आती है
तू नहीं आता लेकिन तेरी याद रोज़ आती है
तेरे लिए इस दिल से फरियाद रोज़ जाती है
बेशक तू ना पढ़ता हो चिट्ठी डाक रोज़ जाती है
बदलता मौसम नहीं इतना जितना तू बदल चुका
कौनसे रूप में बहरूपिया वो ढल चुका
लगता है फिर एक दूसरे शिकार को निकल चुका
हमारा प्रस्ताव वापसी का पैरों में शायद कुचल चुका
यही है दास्तां ए मोहब्बत यही हासिल होता है

बर्बाद जो इस खेल में शामिल होता है
डूबने के बाद यहां किनारा तो क्या सहारा भी नहीं
ना करने वाला दिल से ही इसमें काबिल होता है "- KING IDR

" क्या लगता है खुश हूं मैं?
बिल्कुल भी नहीं।
क्या लगता है नाराज़ हूं?
हां हूं थोड़ा सा।
क्या लगता है तुझ से?
इतना हक़ कहां मिला है मुझे।
क्या लगता है उदास हूं?
हां हूं थोड़ा सा।
क्या लगता है सबको बता दिया?
नहीं बदनाम नहीं कर सकता।
क्या लगता है पता चल गया?
हां थोड़ा सा।
क्या लगता है मिलूंगा कभी?

कभी नहीं तुझ से।
क्या लगता है मेरी गलती?
नहीं कभी नहीं।
क्या लगता है प्यार करूंगा?
नहीं दोस्त।
क्या लगता है हो गया?
कभी नहीं।
क्या लगता है लगाव था?
हां काफी।
क्या लगता है अब करूंगा?
कभी नहीं। "

Dilip M. Bhise

Dilip M. Bhise is a Mumbai-based prolific short story writer and poet at heart. He has shared his writings in many anthologies of WRITERSVILLA, FLAIRS & GLAIRS, UNVOICED HEART, SPOT WRITE, and WORDSGENIX Publications.
His SEVEN anthologies as a co-author are already published:
The short story 'SAM'S UNSPOKEN WORLD' by WRITERSVILLA pub.
The short story 'HARSH REALITY by FLAIRS AND GLAIRS publication
3. Poetry collections 'BOND THAT NEVER ENDS', REMINISCENCE by WRITERS VILLA, and 'LIFE', NANHE FARISHTEY, WINGS OF FANCY.
Presently Junior Lecturer, Department of English, G. D. Goenka International School, Surat, has been teaching (English language and literature) for over a decade. He writes fictional, non-fictional stories, Haikus, and poetry. He loves to rhyme his mind and bask in the warmth of poetry which seems to be the elixir of life for him.

Email: dilipbhise76537611@gmail.com
Instagram ID:- @dilipbhise

On The Qui Vive

It’s not only him but the night is on the qui vive
Stomach much hungry and mouth thirsty but no hee-haw
for that one pop of text set on the mobile screen
That one sign of emoji as a toast to be seen

Mean time reverie takes over and rent the matter with full might,
All naked views and shades of that beautiful face in numerous facets,
Soothing, relieving, satisfying, dimming the craving light
But just for a while until that one pops of much awaited text.

Love illuminates, energizes the world of astir lovers
Their hearts are like beautiful broadcast in the quest
Night seems absolute right, and blessings of the Eros
Irritation and tears in eye balls is purposeful neglect

Sleepless lovers sleep in days and awake all nights
It’s their love wreathing against the haste of life
Better or bitter are no such letters
Harsh or worse is trivial to live life of Lovers

Cognitive Dissonance

Time and again cognitive dissonance
Will I be loved, adored, or cherished
And until when?
My heart pounds over and over again in void cognizance
Will I be loved, adored, or cherished
And until when?

Does material wealth, appearances, or artificiality matters the most?
Or wildness, masculinity, or femininity causes the unrest
Unchangeable cognitive dissonance, detain distant fictions

The way I am, and can not be deciphered still
Will I be loved, adored or, cherished, until when?
Nobody knows but time and openness
And divulging verity
And overt heart executes
No matter the perilous past
Howling present
Fictitious future
Just let the love overwhelmingly take over
Let you be the one's who chooses you
To put silent the cognitive dissonance

Grishma Ninave

Grishma Ninave was born and brought up in the Orange City, Nagpur. She is a Science graduate and an avid reader. Thriller is her favourite genre. Currently working as a Project Head at Flairs & Glairs Publication House. Published in the Editorial section of a national magazine as *Aaj Ki Womaniyaa*, in the first edition of 2021. She won the Be the Change award 2021 organized by OMG book of records. A firm believer that happiness is not something that you find, it's something that you
create. She loves travelling, blogging and listening to music.

Email : ninavegrishma@gmail.com

Instagram ID
@grish_ninave

What Is Life?

My minds travels through
The crests and troughs
That life brings along.

What is life, if not a journey
Of loss and gains
On a road of ups and downs,
And dislocated fragments
Of trust and heartbreaks.

What is life, if not an association
Of love and hatred
And scattered are various emotions,
Conjointly forming a bridge
Between birth and death.

Lead Your Life The Way You Wish

Why do you look around for validation?
When it is going to cause nothing but abberation.
Go ahead and grab your niche,
Lead your life the way you wish...

Crying for the promise that wasn't kept,
Why their flaws do you not accept.
Just make plans and work to accomplish,
Lead your life the way you wish...

Why do you get affected when they look at you pitiably,
One day you too shall be ignorant, probably.
My friend, do not embrace anguish,
Lead your life the way you wish.

It's their fault that they are so subhuman,
But do not cry went to you they abandon.
Negative thoughts from your mind you banish,
Live your life the way you wish.

Ashish Kumar

इनसे मुलाकात कीजिए, आशीष कुमार।ये रायपुर,छत्तीसगढ़ के रहने वाले हैं।वर्तमान में ये तृतीय वर्ष के इंजीनियरिंग स्टूडेंट हैं।
इनका यह मानना है कि जब भी आप अकेलापन महसूस करें,तब अपने कलम को अपना साथी बनाकर अपने मन के सारे जज़्बात भावनाओं के पन्नों में लिखिए,साथ ही लेखन को मन की शांति बताते हुए यह कहते हैं कि लेखन आपको अपने कलम से चीखने का मौका देती है,और बेजुबान को भी शोर देती है।

Mail id- ashishkumarr.718@gmail.com
Ig handle- @teradastoor

तुम- एक अनकही हसीन।

तुम बारिश की वो पहली बूंद सी हो,
शीतल हवाओं की ठंडी सुकून सी हो।

चिलचिलाती धूप की तपन में इक छांव,
और ओस की सिहरन में गुनगुनी धूप सी हो।

उस तपते रेगिस्तान में सूखे गले की आस,
"मरीचिका" ही सही मन की बुझती प्यास सी हो।

काँटों के बीच मुस्कुराती कली सी हो,
भँवरों के बीच महकती "लिली" सी हो।

तुम ही बेचैनी मेरी,तुम ही मेरे चैन हो,
दीदार जिसका करती ये आँखे,तुम ही मेरे दो नैन हो।

सवाल तुम,जवाब भी तुम,हर मूल्य का हिसाब भी तुम,
मेरी शुभकामना,और मेरी अड़चन सी हो।

तुम उस ढ़लती शाम सी खूबसूरत हसीन,
साँसे भी मेरी,और मेरे दिल की धड़कन सी हो।

प्रकृति का दस्तूर।

हर नयी कहानी एक नयी बात सिखाती है
दुनिया के रिवाजों से मन को अवगत कराती है

हर नयी सुबह एक उम्मीद की किरण लेकर आती है
भोर का सूरज मन में एक नयी उमंग भर जाती है

हर वो खुशबू फूलों की खुशी बिखेरकर लाती है
हो चाहे जितनी खूबसूरती मन में सादगी दे जाती है

हर वो चमकते तारे एक ही बात सिखाते हैं
अंधेरों में अपनी तेज चमक बिखेरते चले जाते हैं

हर एक फिजाएं प्रकृति की मन को सुकून दे जाती है
फलों की झुकी डाली विनम्रता की बात सिखाती है

हर दीपक की ज्वाला मन में एक नयी आशा भर जाती है
अंधकार भरी राहों से प्रकाश की ओर ले जाती है

Divyataa Banerjee

She's a sunflower, try not to bring your negative vibes near this Gemini, she believes that you can't be sad forever. A Distinguished Story Teller, Story Writer and Debater. She kills people with success and buries them with a smile.

Email : divyataabanerjee@gmail.com

Instagram ID :-@divyataaaa

Am On My Way.

Dear diary,
I have always written for others, first time in 20 years I am writing something for myself.

Am on my way now, it's been 20 years since I haven't been home, and this has just made me understand the meaning of home, because home is not where you live. It's where your heart resides, where your loved ones are present, it's where you make memories, home is just a house which was initially bricks and mortar, your family members make it a home.

I had a family too, my dad and Bruno. My dad although just a woodcutter was the most lively man ever, he is..I meant. He lives in my heart now. Bruno always created mess but was the closest thing to my heart. The way he licked my face, I still smile thinking about it..*giggles*

Dad was fond of reading, he wanted me to be a writer all his life, he brought books from town and every weekend we had a book party at home, used to read several books in a day!

I still remember the sight- in the middle of the hallway a big window with yellow curtains and the two walls had nothing but the bookshelves with crazy number of books. I wonder how it'll feel to see it now.

20 years ago, dad left me. My long-lost relative got me to town. And here I am, after successfully accomplishing my dad's only wish I am returning to where I belong.

Aunt's house had everything, but it was a house and not a home to me.

By the way, I'll visit Bruno's grave today too.

On the brighter side, am excited. I don't know what to expect, am nervous. So dear diary, I'll continue in a bit...

Dear diary, am back. You won't believe what I just saw. My home was ruined. I cannot put something into words for the first time, dear diary, my home was ruined…

After some days…

Dear diary, I was shook, I didn't know what to write, what I saw was nothing…the shelves had some books, rest all at the floor, the curtains weren't yellow, all turned pale. The blooming trees were dead.

Yes, I didn't go to Bruno's grave. I couldn't. I was weak that day. Today I am my father's daughter. I'll renovate my home, again. Am on my way again

Flairs and Glairs, a platform by a student for the students. We are esteemed youth struggling to carve out our path for our future and we follow a basic mindset Since everyone is not born with all-round skills. Joining hands with people who are born to execute it with perfection is the best way to evolve. Self-Evolution is the need of the hour but, evolving as a community is what we strive for. The initiative as kickstarted by, Founder- Mr. Shubham Shah with the motive to utilize the skillset and talent of writing has now a team of 10+ people who are actively participating into newer forms of learning and discovering talents among youngsters. We Provide platform and services like Publishing opportunities, Open mics, Workshops, Hands-on training. Operating with Brand Name of Flairs and Glairs (Publication House), we offer the chance of elevating a passionate writer to an esteemed author With Brand name Teekhe Zasbaaat. We bring to you an opportunity to get accustomed with the Public Speaking and Presenting of Thoughts along with regular challenges to brush up your inking spirit. The newest initiative to extend our services we introduced in a new writing Platform- The Glittering Fables and Ink Over Tears.

We Choose to Fly Like A Falcon than to be

a Leg Pulling Crab.

To Know More: Infoline – 7781900870
Mail Us At
flairsandglairs@gmail.com / info@flairsandglairs.in
Or Visit is at
www.flairsandglairs.com / www.flairsandglairs.in

Social Handles- @flairsandglairs @teekhezasbaaat

www.ingramcontent.com/pod-product-compliance
Ingram Content Group UK Ltd.
Pitfield, Milton Keynes, MK11 3LW, UK
UKHW022004190726
13853UKWH00004B/1723

9 789391 302542